Stephanie
the Starfish
Fairy

For Natalie Leigh Anderson,
a true friend of the fairies!

Special thanks
to Sue Mongredien

ISBN 978-0-545-28875-0

12 11 10 9 8 7 6   13 14 15 16/0

Printed in the U.S.A.   40

First Scholastic printing, January 2011

Stephanie
the Starfish
Fairy

by Daisy Meadows

SCHOLASTIC INC.

New York   Toronto   London   Auckland
Sydney   Mexico City   New Delhi   Hong Kong

The
Fairyland
Palace

GALA

FAIRYLAND ROYAL AQUARIUM

Fairyland Royal
Aquarium

Kirsty's Gran's
House

Lighthouse

The Park

Tide pool

Ocean Star Sailing Ship

Lea-On-Sea

Whales

Jack Frost's
Ice Castle

Ocean World
Sealife Center

Seals   Dolphins

Baby
Turtles

Leamouth Pier

Penguins

Ice floes

South Pole

With the magic conch shell at my side,
I'll rule the oceans far and wide!
But my foolish goblins have shattered the shell,
So now I cast my icy spell.

Seven shell fragments, be gone, I say,
To the human world to hide away,
Now the shell is gone, it's plain to see,
The oceans will never have harmony!

Contents

Starry Skies   1

Trapped!   13

Searching for Spike   23

Tide Pool Discoveries   31

Shannon to the Rescue   41

Super Stars!   51

Starry Skies

"The ocean sounds so much louder at night, doesn't it?" Kirsty Tate said to her best friend, Rachel Walker. They were making their way down to Leamouth beach in the darkness. Stars twinkled in the sky above them and a full moon cast silvery streaks on the waves.

"It feels completely different at night," Rachel agreed. "No noisy seagulls, no

ice-cream trucks, no families making
sandcastles . . ."

Kirsty smiled. "It's really nice," she said,
hugging herself to
keep warm as
a cool breeze
swept in from
the water.
"Just like
everything else
about this
vacation, really!"

Both girls were staying with Kirsty's
gran for a week during their spring
vacation. Kirsty wasn't exaggerating
when she said they'd been having a great
time. In fact, it had been magical!

The two friends had been helping the

Ocean Fairies look for the seven missing pieces of a magic golden conch shell that had been smashed by Jack Frost's goblins. So far, they'd found four pieces of the shell and had four wonderful fairy adventures. But there were still three more pieces left to find.

Tonight they'd been invited to join Gran's astronomy club for an evening picnic on the beach. The forecast said it was going to be a beautiful, clear night. Gran and her friends had brought card tables and picnic baskets to the beach, plus some impressive-looking telescopes.

Kirsty and Rachel
helped set the
food out as the
guests arrived.
Then, as the sky
grew darker, Gran
pointed out some
of the constellations.
"There are eighty-
eight constellations,
or 'groups of stars',"
she told the girls, and
pointed up. "There's an
easy one—the Great Bear
or, as it's also known, the Big
Dipper. Do you see the shape
of a ladle up there?"

Rachel and Kirsty peered at
where she was pointing. "Yes!"

Rachel cried excitedly. "I see it. There's the handle, and there's the scoop." "Oh, yeah!" Kirsty said, gazing up. "Well, the 'Big Dipper' is part of the Great Bear," Gran explained. "The handle is the bear's tail, and the 'dipper' is part of the bear's body. If you look carefully, you can see legs and the shape

of his head, too." She smiled at the girls through the darkness. "It's a little like connecting the dots to make a picture."

While Gran passed around cups of coffee from her thermos to the adults, Kirsty and Rachel continued to stare at the stars. They tried hard to spot more pictures. "I can see a violin," Rachel said, showing Kirsty. "It's just like Victoria the Violin Fairy's."

"Oh, yes," Kirsty said. "And there's a shoe with ribbons attached, just like Ruby the Red Fairy's!"

An excited cheer went up among the astronomy club members at that moment, and the girls saw that some of them were pointing at the sky.

"A shooting star!" Gran exclaimed. "Well, I never. That's very special. Make a wish, girls!"

"I wish we could meet another Ocean Fairy soon," Rachel murmured at once.

Kirsty heard her. "That's what I wished for, too," she whispered. "We have to find the other pieces of the magic golden conch shell. We only have two days left in Leamouth and there are still three pieces missing!"

The golden conch shell was very important. Every year at a grand oceanside gala, Shannon the Ocean Fairy played a special song on the shell, ensuring order throughout the world's oceans. Before she'd been able to play it this year, though, Jack Frost had sent his goblins to snatch the conch shell from her. He said he didn't like the beach because it was too hot and too noisy, and he didn't see why anyone else should have fun there.

Unfortunately, the goblins had fought over who got to carry the shell. Then they'd dropped it onto the floor, where it smashed into seven pieces. The Ocean Fairies had all tried to grab the broken pieces, but before they could reach them, Jack Frost had cast a spell that sent the shattered shell into the human world. Then he'd vanished.

The fairy queen had used her magic to send each of the Ocean Fairies' special

animal helpers out into the oceans to guard a piece of the broken conch shell. Since then, Kirsty and Rachel had been helping the Ocean Fairies find their animal friends. Each time, the animals had led them to another piece of the shell. But Jack Frost's sneaky goblins were looking for the shell pieces, too. They were desperate to please Jack Frost by finding them before the fairies did.

The shooting star fell now, past the constellations that looked like Victoria's violin and Ruby's shoe. "Here, girls," came a voice. It was one of Gran's friends, a nice old man named Frank. "Would you like to watch the shooting star through this telescope? You'll be able to see it more clearly."

"Yes, please," said Rachel, putting her

eye on the telescope viewer. She started
with excitement as she saw the shooting
star magnified. Only it wasn't actually a
shooting star at all. It was Stephanie the
Starfish Fairy!

Trapped!

"Kirsty, take a look," Rachel said meaningfully, trying very hard not to show how happy she was in front of the astronomers.

Kirsty took her turn at the telescope and peered through the lens. She gasped as she saw what Rachel had noticed. There was

Stephanie, her short red hair blowing in
the wind as she flew. She was wearing

black pants, a
turquoise vest,
and wedge
sandals. She
was heading
right for a
group of
tide pools
farther up the
beach, her tiny body glowing in the
darkness. Was she trying to alert the girls
that she was there, Kirsty wondered?

Rachel smiled to herself, too. She was
sure Stephanie had come to the beach to
look for her starfish, Spike. Hopefully that
meant another piece of the magical shell
was nearby!

"Thank you," Kirsty said politely to Frank, moving away from the telescope. "She—I mean *it*—looks wonderful close-up."

Stephanie's bright light suddenly vanished as she plunged to earth, and the grown-ups returned to their picnic.

"I think we should investigate," Kirsty murmured to Rachel. "Come on, let's ask my gran if we can take a walk."

Kirsty's gran was helping herself to a plate of sandwiches. "Of course you can go exploring," she said, when the girls asked. "You both have flashlights, right?

Just be careful where you walk. The seaweed might be slippery. Stay away from the water's edge—and don't go too far."

"We won't," Rachel promised. The girls hurried away, shining their flashlights along the beach. "I wonder where Stephanie is," she said to Kirsty, once they were a safe distance from the grown-ups. A cloud had slipped over the moon, making the beach seem much darker.

The girls ran their flashlights over the sand and rocks, but couldn't see any sign of the little fairy.

"I hope she didn't fall *in* one of the tide pools," Kirsty said anxiously. "She'd be in trouble if her wings got soggy. She wouldn't be able to fly!"

She and Rachel were just starting to worry when Stephanie's sparkly light reappeared. "Oh, there she is!" Rachel gasped excitedly. "I wonder why she's shining like that though."

The two friends stared at the little fairy's bright light zipping around frantically in all directions. "I think she's just letting us know where she is," Kirsty replied. "Come on, let's shine our lights over there so we can see her better."

She and Rachel both held out their lights and tilted them

so that the beams illuminated Stephanie.
In dismay, they realized why the fairy
was thrashing around. She'd been caught
in a tide pool net—held by a goblin!

"Oh, no," Rachel whispered. "Come
on, we've got to help her!"

They ran toward Stephanie and the
goblin, but soon saw that he wasn't alone.
There were *three*
goblins, all
dressed in
black with
brown
camouflage
blotches on
their faces.
The camouflage
had made them very hard to see in
the dark.

"What are those lights?" one of the goblins asked, blinking as the flashlights lit up his face. "I can't see anything with them in my eyes."

"Move away from them then, silly," another goblin snapped. "Hurry up and tie that net before the fairy escapes."

"Help!" cried Stephanie, still fighting to get out. "Help me!"

The girls rushed over, but they were too late. One of the goblins used a long piece of seaweed to tie up the top of the net. Stephanie was trapped!

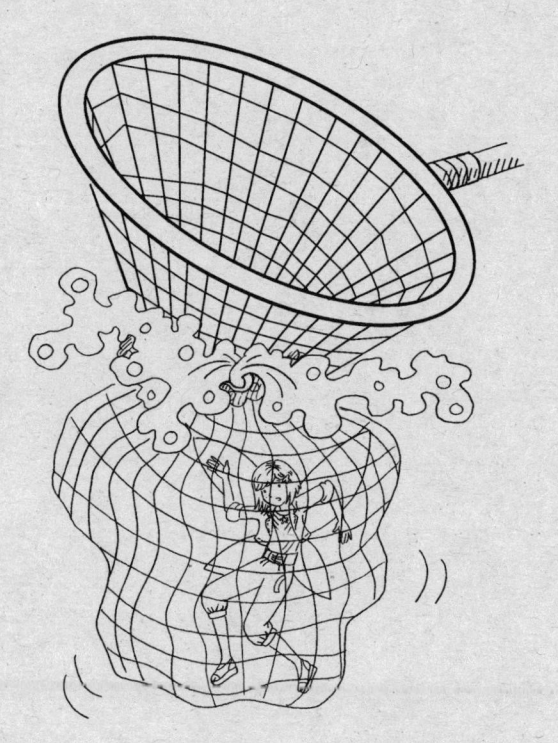

Searching for Spike

Alarmed, Rachel and Kirsty snapped off their lights and ducked down behind the rocks, just out of sight. Stephanie was giving off just enought light for them to see the goblins carrying the net around the tide pools. They held it above the water and peered down. "She is the *star*fish fairy, I suppose," Kirsty thought out loud. "Maybe she always shines like a star?"

"Yes, and now the goblins are using her light to help them hunt for Spike, I bet," Rachel realized, her heart thumping. It was horrible to see poor Stephanie swinging around so helplessly in that net.

"We've got to get her out of there," Kirsty muttered, "and somehow find Spike before the goblins do. Let me think. . . ."

Before the girls could come up with a good plan, they both noticed a pink sparkly light coming from a nearby pool. The goblins spotted it, too. "Aha! That must be the starfish!" They cheered and rushed over.

Rachel felt tense as she watched them searching. "Where is it?" the goblins grumbled. "Silly starfish, we saw you sparkling. We know you're over here somewhere!"

"I don't see anything," one of them muttered angrily after they'd splashed around for a while. "We must have been seeing things."

"There's a different sparkly light!" another goblin yelled, sounding

happier. "Maybe *that's* the starfish."

The goblins hurried over to another pool. Kirsty and Rachel could see a faint shimmering coming from underneath the water. But as soon as the goblins reached the pool, this light vanished just like the last one.

"I wonder if that really is Spike," Kirsty whispered to Rachel as the goblins hunted without success. "I'm starting to think  that Stephanie is making those lights with fairy magic to fool the goblins!"

Rachel nodded. "I bet you're right,"

she said. "Good for her. While she's keeping them busy running around after the different lights, we should try to find Spike ourselves. Where should we look first?"

"Hmmm," said Kirsty. "Well, my guess is that Stephanie was heading straight for Spike before she was captured." She gazed up at the stars. "She went past the violin shape, didn't she? And then past Ruby's shoe . . ." She paused, staring at the sky in surprise. "I don't remember *that* constellation, do you?"

Rachel looked up at the pattern of stars Kirsty had spotted next to the shoe. "Your gran said it was like connecting the dots, didn't she?" Rachel said, trying to figure out the picture in this new constellation. Then she gave a squeak

of excitement as she realized what it was. "A starfish! It's a clue!" Kirsty grinned. "Stephanie must have used her fairy magic to make it," she said happily. "She's showing us where she thinks Spike is—and hopefully where another piece of the conch shell is, too. Let's go!"

The girls crept over to the tide pool directly underneath the starfish constellation. They had to be quiet so the goblins didn't see or hear them. Thankfully, the goblins had been led to yet another sparkly light in the opposite direction. They were busily splashing around over there, moaning about how much they hated getting wet.

As Kirsty and Rachel reached the tide pool, the moon slid out from behind the clouds again. Suddenly, it was much easier to see what they were doing. They could see mussel shells and barnacles around the edge of the pool and—hooray! Right at the edge of the shallow water, pulsing with a faint pink light, was a starfish. "Ooh," Rachel whispered excitedly. "Spike, is that you?"

Tide Pool Discoveries

The girls peered closely at the pinkish yellow starfish lying in the pool. They grinned as it lifted up one arm and gave them a little wave.

"So it *is* you, Spike," Kirsty said happily. "Yay!" She put a hand in the pool to pick him up and Spike hopped into her palm. "I wonder where the shell is? Have you been guarding it, Spike?"

Previously, when they'd found the magic ocean creatures, their fairy friends had been there to translate for them. This time, the girls would have to figure it out on their own. Spike wriggled on Kirsty's hand as if he wanted desperately to tell her something. "What do you think he wants us to know?" Rachel wondered.

"It's too bad Stephanie isn't here to tell us what he's saying," Kirsty said.

Just then, Rachel caught a glimpse of

something golden hidden under some seaweed in the tide pool. "Oh," she said, lifting up the seaweed. "It's the shell!"

The mussels in the pool began opening and closing their own shells as if they were applauding. Spike seemed to dance a little jig of joy on Kirsty's hand.

Rachel beamed as she scooped up the golden piece of conch shell. This was the fifth piece they'd found!

"This is great," Kirsty said happily. "We've found Spike *and* the shell! Now we just need to rescue Stephanie so she can take them both back to Fairyland."

She and Rachel glanced over to where Stephanie was still using her fairy magic to cast sparkles in the pools to trick the goblins. "The lights she's making look fainter to me," Rachel said anxiously. "Oh, no. She must be very tired by now, with all the magic she's used," Kirsty

said. "What should we do?"

Rachel thought for a moment. The goblins were sounding more and more bad-tempered as they continued to hunt for Spike. They would get even angrier if she and Kirsty tried to rescue Stephanie. If only they had someone to help them!

Then an idea came to Rachel. "We could use our lockets to go to Fairyland and ask for help," she suggested. She grabbed the pretty locket that hung around her neck. The fairy king and queen had given one to both Rachel and Kirsty, and

they contained fairy dust that could take them to Fairyland.

"Good idea," Kirsty said. She opened her locket and sprinkled fairy dust over herself. She scattered some of the glittering dust over Spike, too, and then she and Rachel held hands. Usually, a sparkly whirlwind came and whisked them away to Fairyland.

But nothing happened this time. "That's strange," Rachel said. "Maybe it only works in daylight."

"Maybe we didn't use enough," Kirsty said. She sprinkled another pinch of dust over herself. But still nothing happened.

Spike squirmed on her hand and Kirsty glanced down at him. "I wonder if it's because Spike's not with Stephanie?" she said to Rachel. "Maybe the magic won't let us take him or the shell back

without Stephanie." She bit her lip. "Looks like we'll have to leave them both behind while we go get help."

"We'll hide you very carefully, Spike," Rachel said, as Kirsty lowered him back into the pool. "And we'll hide the piece of shell, too."

The girls tucked Spike and the golden piece of conch into a group of anemones. They were the exact same shade of pink as Spike, and their waving fronds closed around him. It seemed like they knew they had to keep him and the shell out of sight.

The moment the girls finished, a

whirlwind sparkling with twinkling stars whipped up around them. They were off to Fairyland!

Shannon to the Rescue

A few seconds later, Rachel and Kirsty felt themselves being lowered gently to the ground, and the whirlwind vanished. They looked around to see that they were in Fairyland. The whirlwind had brought them right to the Royal Aquarium where their Ocean Fairy adventures had all begun!

Sitting outside the aquarium was
Shannon the Ocean Fairy herself, her
wings drooping sadly. She jumped up,
looking much more cheerful when she
saw the girls
nearby. "Oh,
hello!" she called.
"Have you found
another piece of
the golden conch?"

"Yes, we have,"
Rachel replied, "*and*
we've found Spike. But
there's a problem."
She and Kirsty explained
that Stephanie had been captured by the
goblins and was being held prisoner in
their fishing net. "Stephanie seems really
tired now, and we're worried about her,"

Kirsty finished. "Will you help us rescue her?"

Shannon nodded. "Of course," she replied. "Let's go to Leamouth!"

Shannon waved her wand and a whirlwind appeared, pulling the three

of them up into the air. It spun faster
and faster until everything was a blur of
rainbow colors and glitter. Moments later,
they were back in Leamouth—but Kirsty
and Rachel weren't their usual human
selves any more. Shannon had turned
them into fairies! They each had beautiful
sparkling wings on their backs.

"Down here," Shannon cried, darting
behind a large rock. "Oh!" she said
in surprise.

Kirsty and Rachel flew quickly after her, wondering what she'd found. "Puffins!" exclaimed Rachel, recognizing the comical-looking black-and-white birds. "I've never seen a real one before!"

Shannon frowned. "I've certainly never

seen them at *night* before," she replied, before flying up to the biggest puffin. "Guys, you're supposed to be asleep now, not wandering around on the beach!" She shook her head. "This is because the golden conch shell is still broken," she told Rachel and Kirsty. "The ocean creatures are all mixed up. The sooner we can fix the shell and I can play my ocean song on it, the better."

Kirsty glanced around for the goblins.

"There they are," she said, spotting them nearby. "And there's Stephanie in the net. Can you see her?" The silvery moon above them cast just enough light to show poor Stephanie lying at the bottom of the goblins' net. "Oh, dear," Shannon said. "I'm so glad you came to me for help, girls. She does need rescuing—and fast! Let me think. . . ."

Her pretty face scrunched into a frown as she tried to come up with a plan. Rachel and Kirsty thought hard, too. It was difficult to concentrate with the puffin family shuffling around, pecking at the seaweed, and making soft squawking noises to each other.

Then Shannon grinned. "It's lucky that the puffins are here, actually. They might just be able to help us out."

"What do you mean?" Rachel asked.

"I mean, let's set a trap," Shannon said, still smiling. "We'll get the ocean creatures to join in. If we all work together, I'm sure we can stop those goblins!"

Super Stars!

A few minutes later, Kirsty, Rachel, and Shannon had everything ready to go. "I'll use my magic to make a pink glow in this tide pool, so the goblins think I'm Spike," Shannon reminded the girls.

"Then we'll try to tempt them over," Kirsty giggled. "Aren't they in for a nice surprise?"

She and Rachel flew through the darkness to where the goblins were searching for Spike in yet another tide pool. "I think we already looked in this one," one of them complained. "I'm tired of this! If I have to touch one more slimy piece of seaweed, I'll—"

"Hi there, having fun?" Rachel asked sweetly as she and Kirsty hovered in midair above their heads.

"You!" the goblin shouted, his eyes gleaming furiously. "What are you doing here? Don't you know what happens to meddling fairies? We catch them!" He held up the net with Stephanie inside it as a warning.

"Ahh, but we can help you," Kirsty said. "We know where the magic starfish *and* the piece of conch shell are. We'll tell you, if you want."

"The only thing is," Rachel added, "we need you to give us our friend in exchange. Do we have a deal?"

The goblins laughed at this. "Yeah, right," the tallest one said, scowling. "We're not falling for your fairy tricks. You can have your friend back *after* we've found the shell piece, but not before."

Just then, his friend elbowed him. "Hey, look!" he said, pointing to the tide pool where Shannon was hiding. A bright pink light was streaming from it. He turned back to the fairies with a triumphant look. "Ha! We don't need your deals," he said. "We can find the starfish and the shell all by ourselves!"

With that, the goblins rushed gleefully toward the glowing tide pool.

Kirsty put two fingers between her lips and blew a piercing whistle. That was the signal for the fun to start!

As the goblins ran across the sand, they were suddenly surrounded by the puffin family. The puffins flew at them, squawking and snapping their great beaks. The goblins were terrified!

"Help! It's a bird monster!" one of them yelped, trying to dodge a puffin who was nipping at his ankle. "Run faster!"

Swerving and stumbling, the goblins finally made it past the puffins. But moments later, they came on a whole horde of crabs who jabbed at the goblins' legs with their sharp pincers.

"*Ow! Ow! Ow!* What's going on?" the goblins cried in terror. "The beach is full of monsters!"

Two of the goblins managed to get
away, but a large
red crab had a
tight hold on the
other goblin's
big toe and was
pinching it for all
he was worth. This
goblin had to sit down and try to wrestle
the crab off.

"That stopped one of them," Kirsty said,
watching with glee. "The plan is working
perfectly!"

Next, the goblins had to climb over
some other tide pools to get to where
Shannon was. But one of the goblins was
rushing, tripped over a large lumpy rock,
and fell smack onto some seaweed.

Before he could move, the crowd of
puffins rushed up and circled him. They
began pecking at him all over again.
"Ow!" he cried. "Go away! Shoo!"

"That's two down . . ." Rachel said,
smiling as the puffins showed no sign
of letting the goblin go anywhere.
"The goblin who's left is the one with
Stephanie. Let's hope the last part of the
plan works."

The goblin with the net began climbing

around the next tide pool. He still seemed
intent on finding Spike and the conch
shell piece. But Shannon had asked the
ocean snails and sea sponges to make the
rocks around this pool extra slippery. The
goblin soon found it very tricky to keep
his balance.

"*Whooooaaa!*" he cried, skidding and
sliding, his arms waving in the air.
"*Heeelllppp!*"

On his very next step, he skidded right into the tide pool and the net went flying out of his grasp. *"Yuck!"* he wailed as he splashed into the water. "I'm covered in smelly seaweed!"

Rachel and Kirsty went diving to catch
the net, and so did Shannon, flying out
of her hiding place in the last tide pool.
Between the three of them, they grabbed
on to it, and
lowered it gently
to the ground.
Then they untied
the top of the net
and Stephanie
fluttered out,
looking pale and
tired, but relieved
to be free.

"Thank you, all of you," she said,
hugging them each in turn. "It's so good
to be out of that awful net!"

"We found Spike and the piece of conch

shell," Rachel told her excitedly. "Come and see!"

They led Stephanie over to the pool where the anemones were still hiding Spike and the shell from sight. As soon as he saw his fairy friend, Spike gave a happy wriggle all over.

Stephanie touched Spike lightly with her wand. He shrank down to fairy-size and leaped into her arms.

Then Shannon waved her wand over Kirsty and Rachel, who turned back into regular size girls again. "Thank you so

much." She smiled. "I'm so happy that
we have another piece of the conch shell.
Stephanie and I will shrink this
and take it back to Fairyland."

"Good-bye, and
thanks again,"
Stephanie said.
"Oh, and enjoy
the stars!"

With a last
flurry of fairy
dust, she, Spike,
and Shannon were
gone.

"Enjoy the stars?" Rachel echoed
as she and Kirsty made their way back
to Gran and her friends. "What did she
mean by that?"

"She must have known we were here with the astronomy club, I guess," Kirsty replied. "Look, there's Gran now. Hello!" she called, as they reached the group of stargazers.

Kirsty's gran was offering around a tray of cookies and she smiled at the girls. "Just in time for a treat," she said. "Take a few each, there are plenty."

The cookies were all different shapes and sizes, and Kirsty smiled as she noticed several that were in the shape of a star. Remembering Stephanie's words, Kirsty

deliberately picked a star-shaped cookie, and so did Rachel. "Just like the shooting star," Gran chuckled. "I hope your wishes come true, girls." Kirsty and Rachel smiled at each other as Gran bustled away. "They already *did* come true," Rachel said. Kirsty bit into her cookie. "Yum," she said. "I'm *definitely* going to enjoy these stars!"

THE OCEAN FAIRIES

Stephanie the Starfish Fairy has
found her piece of the golden conch shell!
Now Rachel and Kirsty must help . . .

Whitney
the Whale Fairy!

Join their next underwater adventure
in this special sneak peek. . . .

All Aboard the Ocean Star

"This is so much fun, Kirsty!" Rachel
Walker called to her best friend, Kirsty
Tate, as their ship, the *Ocean Star*, bobbed
across the waves. "Look, can you see that
school of fish?"

Kirsty peered over the ship's railing and
saw a group of tiny, silvery fish darting
through the sparkling turquoise water.
Some of the other girls and boys on the

boat trip rushed over to look, too.

"Leamouth looks so pretty in the sunshine, doesn't it?" Kirsty remarked, as they sailed across the bay. She and Rachel stood on the deck of the *Ocean Star*, enjoying the view of the seaside resort. From here they could see a long stretch of golden beach and whitewashed cottages clustered around the harbor.

"Ahoy there, sailors!" Captain Andy shouted, waving at the girls and boys on the deck below him. He stood behind the wooden ship's wheel, turning it back and forth to guide the boat through the water. "If you'd visited Leamouth hundreds of years ago, the harbor would have been full of large sailing ships just like the *Ocean Star*. There was one very famous boat called the *Mermaid*, but sadly it sank somewhere around this area a very long time ago."

"Do you know where the wreck is, Captain Andy?" asked Thomas, one of the boys on the trip.

Captain Andy shook his head. "We don't know exactly where the ship sank," he replied. "It had a beautiful carved and painted figure of a mermaid attached to its front. Legend says that the mermaid statue now watches over this area from wherever the wreck lies on the bed of the ocean."

"What a great story," Rachel remarked to Kirsty. "It sounds like magic!"

Suddenly Thomas gave a cry. "What's *that?*" he shouted, pointing at the foamy waves ahead of them. "I can see something moving."

"Wow!" Captain Andy exclaimed. "The *Mermaid* has certainly brought us good luck today. Look everyone, there are whales!"

"Oh!" Rachel gasped with delight. "Oh, Kirsty, aren't they *beautiful*?"

"They're gorgeous!" Kirsty was breathless with excitement, her eyes glued to her binoculars.

Just then, Kirsty noticed another, smaller whale leap out of the water behind the others. Kirsty caught her breath as she noticed a faint glimmer of silver sparkles around the whale.

"Rachel, look!" Kirsty whispered. "That whale at the back is glowing with fairy magic. I think it's one of the magic ocean creatures. That must mean a piece of the golden conch shell is nearby!"

Perfectly Princess

Don't miss these royal adventures!

Printed on colored pages!